To the Head Start kids
in Tanana: Have fun learning
about Alaska animals with
songs and chants!

Alice Wright

Alaska Animals, We Love You!

Chants and Poems for Children

Written by
LaVon Bridges and Alice Wright

Illustrated and Designed by
M.R. Anderson

* See Appendix for ostinatos
and melody notation.
CD contains all selections

Publication Consultants
Since 1978

PO Box 221974 Anchorage, Alaska 99522-1974

Table of Contents

Poems and Chants:

Appendix of Melodies and/or Ostinatos:

ISBN 1-59433-028-X

Library of Congress Catalog Card Number: 2005901983

Copyright 2005 by LaVon Bridges and Alice Wright
—First Printing 2005—
—Second Printing 2006—

* indicates to look in appendix.
Listen to CD to understand how to perform.
CD contains all selections.

Printed in Thailand

Dedication

To the children of Alaska. Many of these children have enjoyed the chants and poems in this book as they have learned to speak and read English. In addition, this work is dedicated to the extraordinary classroom teachers everywhere. May they continue to enjoy the rhythm and rhymes of these chants and poems as they help students discover Alaska animals.

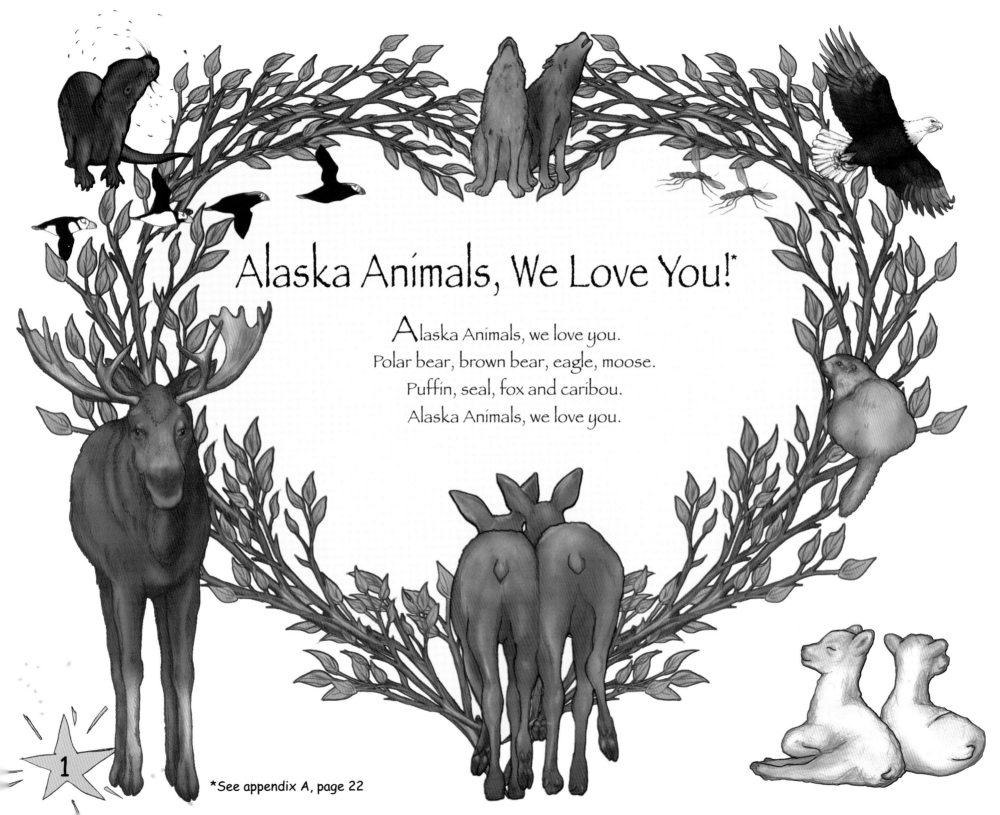

Alaska Animals, We Love You!*

Alaska Animals, we love you.
Polar bear, brown bear, eagle, moose.
Puffin, seal, fox and caribou.
Alaska Animals, we love you.

1

*See appendix A, page 22

I see the claws on a polar bear, polar bear.
Do you see a polar bear? He's so white.

I see the antlers on a moose, a moose.
Do you see a moose? He's so big.

I see the wings on an eagle, an eagle.
Do you see an eagle? He's so strong.

I see the whiskers on a seal, a seal.
Do you see a seal? He's so slippery.

I see the tail on a fox, a fox.
Do you see a fox? He's so sly.

Alaska Animals, we love you.
Polar bear, brown bear, eagle, moose.
Puffin, seal, fox and caribou.
Alaska Animals, we love you.

2

Ostinato: Polar bear, Brown bear, Black bear, Grizzly

Can you let a polar bear sit down in your favorite chair?
Can you let a polar bear sit down in your favorite chair?

No, he likes to sit on ice, for he thinks that snow is nice.
No, he likes to sit on ice, for he thinks that snow is nice.

Can a brown bear ride your bike?
Can a brown bear ride your bike?

If he does, go take a hike.
If he does, go take a hike.

Can a black bear ride the bus?
Can a black bear ride the bus?

Yes, if he won't make a fuss.
Yes, if he won't make a fuss.

Can a grizzly catch a fish?
Can a grizzly catch a fish?

Yes, and he won't need a dish.
Yes, and he won't need a dish.

Bears

Mr. Marmot, gray and furry,
sleeping in the winter
through the arctic night.
Napping on a mountain slope,
waiting for the light.

Mr. Marmot

When you wake to summer sun,
on your short legs you will run.
Gathering grass will be such fun!

When autumn snow begins to fly,
you'll swish your tail and whistle, "Bye,"
to find your burrow warm and deep.
Then dressed in fur, you'll go to sleep.

4

"I see a beaver in the stream!
I see a beaver!" I did scream.
He's by his house; he's by his dam.
He's a builder, like a man.

"I see a beaver in the stream!
I see a beaver!" I did scream.
He has big teeth; he chews down trees.
He tunnels up, you can see.

A Beaver

"I see a beaver in the stream!
I see a beaver!" I did scream.
He's a rodent; he's a mammal.
He's a wonder, nice and gentle.

"I see a beaver in the stream!
I see a beaver!" I did scream.
He swims in water; he has nice fur.
When he slaps his tail, he's a blur.

5

Caríbou

Ostinato: Caribou, Caribou

Oh, you caribou, so many in a herd,
dropping calves on open plains,
need to be alert.

Oh, you caribou, so many in a herd,
here come the grizzlies;
don't you think they'll hurt?

Oh, you caribou, so many in a herd,
here come the wolves;
they'll eat you with a smirk.

Oh, you caribou, so many in a herd,
here come mosquitoes;
in water you'll submerge.

Oh, you caribou, so many in a herd,
here come ice and snow;
for lichen you will search.

There's a Wolf

There's a wolf a-howling on the tundra.
He's calling to his mate on the tundra.
I hear him call; I see his paw.
The wolf is howling on the tundra. (howl)

There's a wolf a-howling on the mountain.
He's gathering his pack on the mountain.
I hear him yip; I see his lip.
The wolf is howling on the mountain. (howl)

There's a wolf a-howling in the forest.
He's protecting the pups in the forest.
I hear him snuff; I see his ruff.
The wolf is howling in the forest. (howl)

There's a wolf a-howling on the seashore.
He's an alpha wolf on the seashore.
I hear him breathe; I see him leave.
The wolf is howling on the seashore. (howl)

owoooo

*See appendix B, page 23

Wolves

We are the Denali Park Wolves

We stay in the pack, Jack.
We eat good food, Dude.
We help each other, Brother.
We work together, Heather.
We like to howl, Pal!
OWOOooo.

We are very smart, Bart.
Each one is unique, Zeke.
We obey our leader, Peter.
Together we are strong, Wong.
We like to howl, Pal!
OWOOooo.

We're always alert, Bert.
We keep peace in the clan, Stan.
We like to communicate, Mate.
We run faster than moose, Duce
We like to howl, Pal!
OWOOooo.

*See appendix C, page 24

There's a Moose in the Woods!

There's a moose in the woods.
There's a moose loose in the woods.
There's a moose running loose in the woods!
He's jumping the logs and swimming the lakes.
Stay out of his way, for goodness sakes!
There's a moose running loose in the woods!

9

Muskox

Oomingmak

Ostinato: Muskox, Oomingmak

Muskox.
Bearded one.
Standing in a circle,
guarding cows and little calves
from a wolf attack.
Muskox.
Bearded one.
Standing in a circle.

10

Ostinato: Otter, Otter,

swimming in the water

Otters

See the little otters
swimming in the water,
munching on mussels,
crabs and fish.

Watch them wrestle,
romp and slide
down the muddy slopes
and icy riverside.

11

Where Have All the Otters Gone?

Where have all the otters gone?
There were many here before.

Where have all the otters gone?
Did hunters raid the store?

Where have all the otters gone?
Did careless men spill oil?

Where have all the otters gone?

Dall Sheep *
(To the tune of Baa, Baa, Black Sheep)

Baa, baa, Dall sheep.
Have you any lambs?
Yes sir, yes sir,
three little lambs.

One to run and hide.
One to stay with me.
And one to run
up and down
the mountain side with glee.

Baa, baa, Dall sheep.
Have you any lambs?
Yes sir, yes sir,
three little lambs.

*See appendix D, page 25

13

Belugas

I saw a pod of belugas
swimming in the bay.
I watched the whales swim swiftly past,
going where, I cannot say.
They travel in another world,
a world unknown to me.
It is a vast, enormous place
we call the deep blue sea.

Ptarmigan

Ptarmigan, ptarmigan,
build your nest, on the ground, on the ground.

Ptarmigan, ptarmigan,
line your nest with leaves and grass, leaves and grass.

Ptarmigan, ptarmigan,
please turn white from black and brown, black and brown.

Ptarmigan, ptarmigan,
Like the snow on the ground, on the ground.

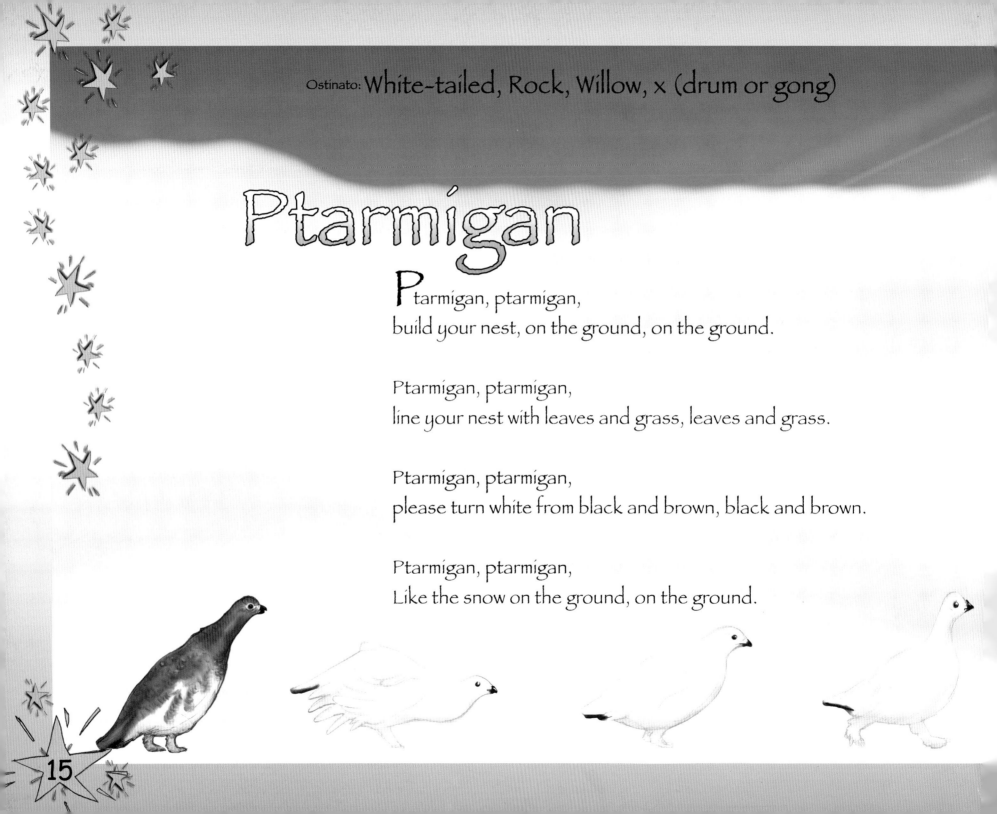

Willow Ptarmigan

Willow ptarmigan,
Alaska's state bird,
has a black tail, I've heard.

Willow ptarmigan,
Alaska's state bird,
turns brown in summer, I've heard.

Willow ptarmigan,
Alaska's state bird,
lives in scrub, I've heard.

Willow ptarmigan,
Alaska's state bird,
turns white in winter, I've heard.

Willow ptarmigan,
black tail, brown in summer,
lives in scrub, white in winter, I've heard.

Eagles

Eagles flying in the sky,

soaring,

soaring,

oh, so high!

I will watch the eagles fly,

climbing,

climbing,

in the sky.

When the eagles come to rest,
they will build a great, big nest.

Ostinato: Who... uh, Who... uh, Who... uh, Who... uh

The Snowy Owl

Do you hear the Snowy Owl,
wild, wise and curious fowl?

Asking questions in the night,
from the hill, with moon so bright.

Watching for a hare or mouse,
or is he guarding a lemming's house?

Snowy Owl

Snowy Owl, great big owl, sitting on a pingaluk.

Looking right at you, looking right at me.

Snowy Owl, great big owl, sitting on a hill.

18

A Puffin

On the rock there is a puffin.
What, a muffin?
No, a puffin!

The Puffin

Ostinato: Tufted puffin, Horned puffin

The puffin is unique
with an orange and yellow beak.
He likes to swim and dive.
He catches fish alive.

He makes his rookery high
among the crags and rocks,
where he can hide quite well
from his enemy the fox.

19

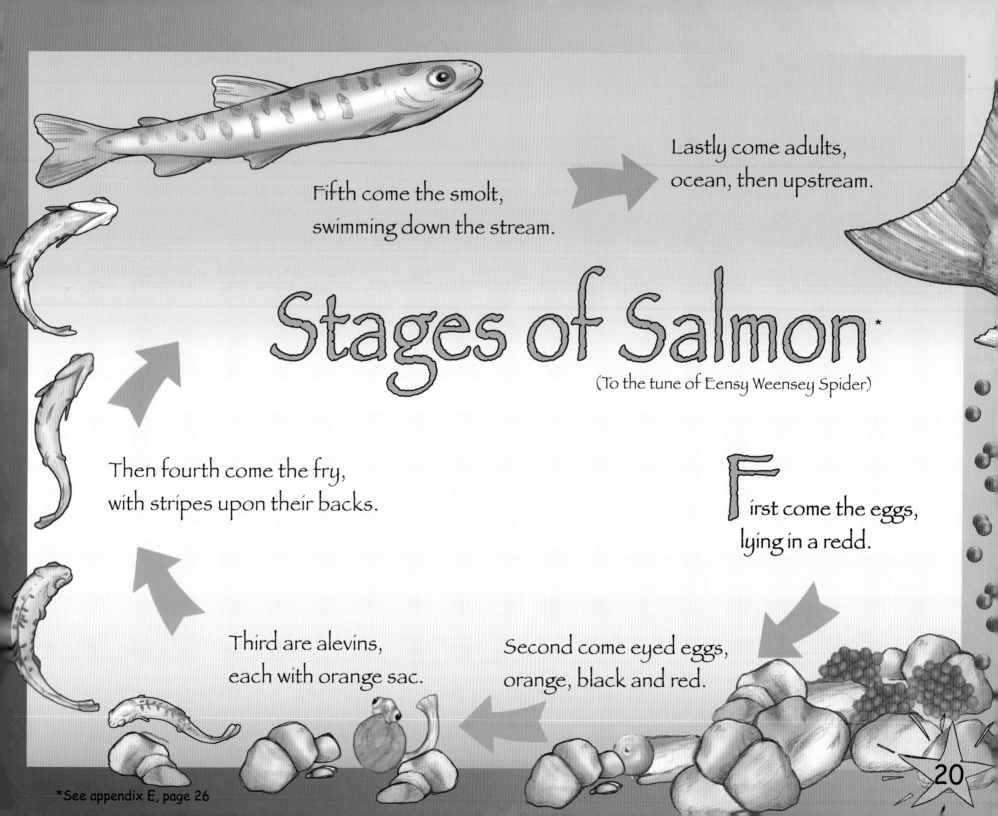

Fifth come the smolt,
swimming down the stream.

Lastly come adults,
ocean, then upstream.

Stages of Salmon*

(To the tune of Eensy Weensey Spider)

Then fourth come the fry,
with stripes upon their backs.

First come the eggs,
lying in a redd.

Third are alevins,
each with orange sac.

Second come eyed eggs,
orange, black and red.

*See appendix E, page 26

Spring in Alaska

Moose are running.
Bears are coming.
Sheep are climbing,
climbing,
climbing.

Sun is shining.
Geese are flying.
Snow is melting,
melting,
melting.

Alaska Animals, We Love You!

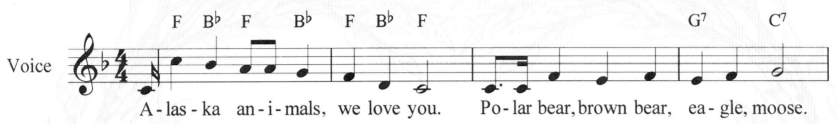

Voice

A-las-ka an-i-mals, we love you. Po-lar bear, brown bear, ea-gle, moose.

Voice

Puf - fin, seal, fox and car - i - bou. A - las - ka an - i - mals, we love you.

Spoken:

I see the claws on a polar bear, polar bear.
Do you see a polar bear? He's so white!

I see the antlers on a moose, a moose.
Do you see a moose? He's so big!

I see the wings on an eagle, an eagle.
Do you see an eagle? He's so strong!

I see the whiskers on a seal, a seal.
Do you see a seal? He's so slippery!

I see the tail on a fox, a fox.
Do you see a fox? He's so sly!

Repeat melody (above)

22

There's a Wolf

Melody

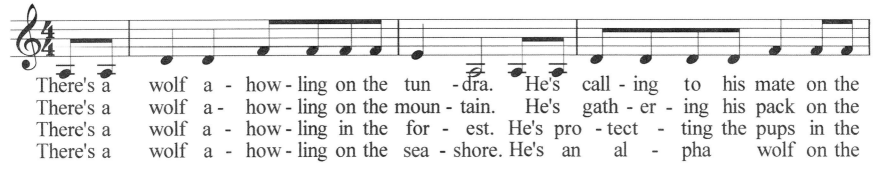

There's a wolf a - how - ling on the tun - dra. He's call - ing to his mate on the
There's a wolf a - how - ling on the moun - tain. He's gath - er - ing his pack on the
There's a wolf a - how - ling in the for - est. He's pro - tect - ting the pups in the
There's a wolf a - how - ling on the sea - shore. He's an al - pha wolf on the

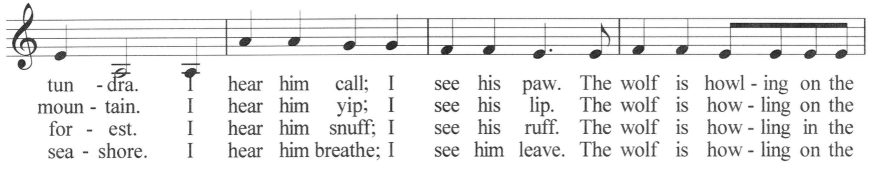

tun - dra. I hear him call; I see his paw. The wolf is howl - ing on the
moun - tain. I hear him yip; I see his lip. The wolf is how - ling on the
for - est. I hear him snuff; I see his ruff. The wolf is how - ling in the
sea - shore. I hear him breathe; I see him leave. The wolf is how - ling on the

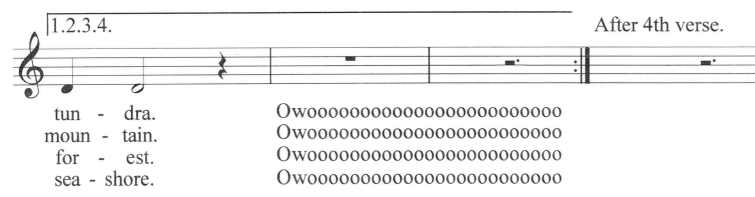

1.2.3.4.   After 4th verse.

tun - dra.   Owooooooooooooooooooooooooooo
moun - tain.   Owooooooooooooooooooooooooooo
for - est.   Owooooooooooooooooooooooooooo
sea - shore.   Owooooooooooooooooooooooooooo

23

Ostinatos for use with "There's a Wolf" and "We are the Denali Park Wolves"

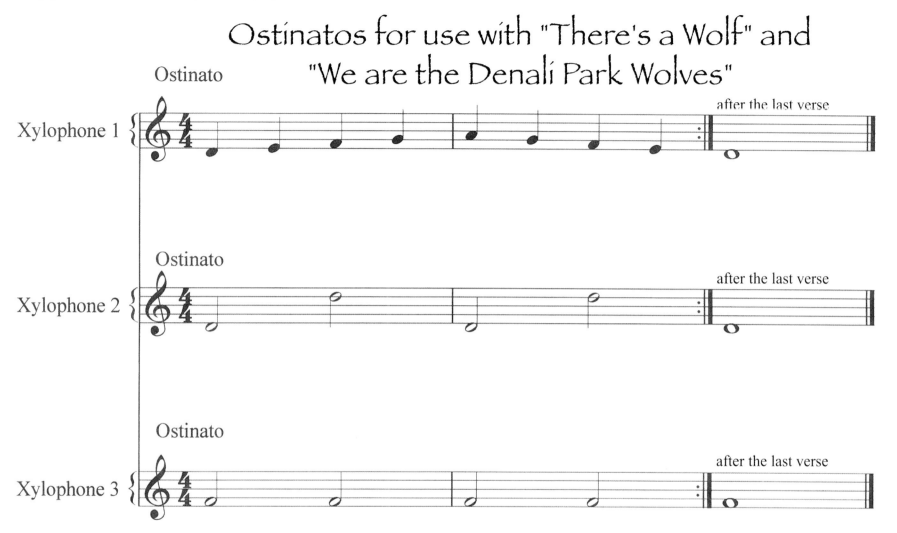

Dall Sheep

Stages of Salmon

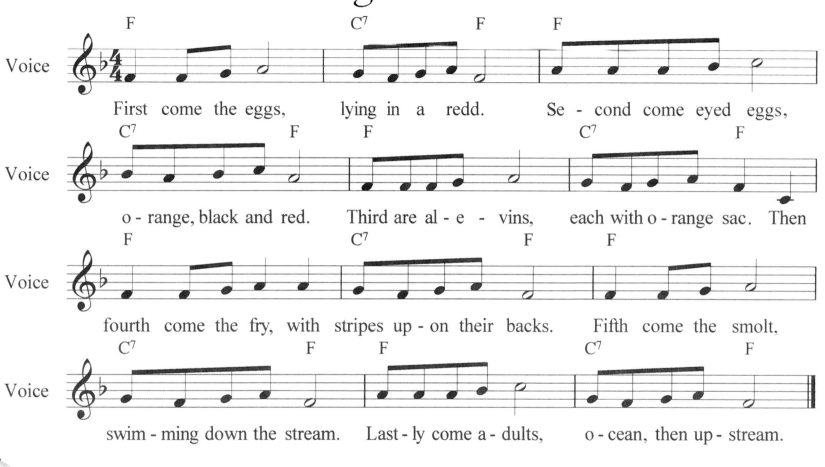

First come the eggs, lying in a redd. Se - cond come eyed eggs,

o - range, black and red. Third are al - e - vins, each with o - range sac. Then

fourth come the fry, with stripes up - on their backs. Fifth come the smolt,

swim - ming down the stream. Last - ly come a - dults, o - cean, then up - stream.

26

Glossary

Alevin - refers to a developmental stage of salmon. This is the third stage, after egg and eyed egg.

Arctic - pronounced AHRK tihk or AHR tihk, is the area of continuous cold around the North Pole. The Arctic includes the Arctic Ocean, as well as thousands of islands, and the northern parts of the continents of Europe, Asia and North America.

Beluga - is a small, toothed whale with a round head. Although most live in the Arctic, some are found farther south. Belugas eat fish, squid, crab, and shrimp. Belugas are white or yellowish. Babies are gray. Sometimes they seem to smile.

Chant - in this book, a poem said out loud, usually by a group, often with an ostinato.

Denali - is part of the Alaska Range. Denali, which means The Great One or The High One, was named by the Athabaskan people.

Fry - small adolescent fish.

Lemming - is a small plump rodent, related to the mouse. Lemmings live in the northern, cold parts of the world.

Lichen - pronounced LY kuhn, is an organism that is really two organisms: an alga and a fungus living together as a single unit. The alga can make food with the help of sunshine, while the fungus cannot make food, but absorbs water rapidly.

Marmot - pronounced MAHR muht, is the largest animal of the squirrel family. These rodents live in burrows, and are found in much of the Northern Hemisphere.

Muskox - is a large, hairy wild ox that lives in the cold plains of the Arctic. It defends itself against cold weather with its thick overcoat. Its dark, shaggy hair is the longest of any mammal.

Mussel - pronounced MUHS uhl, is a water animal protected by a hard shell. Mussels live in oceans and in fresh water. Each shell has two plates called valves, which are joined by a hinge. The shell closes tight if a predator comes near.

Oomingmak - is an Inupiaq word for "muskox" and means "bearded one". It is pronounced OOM ing mock.

Ostinato - a musical or verbal pattern heard repeatedly throughout a composition. In this book, the ostinatos are "chanted" with the poems, or played on xylophones.

Pingaluk - This is a small pingo, or frost heave, on which the snowy owl lays eggs. The word comes from the Inupiaq language.

Ptarmigan - pronounced TAR mi gun, is a bird which has short feathers on its feet to help it travel across the snow. In winter, its feathers are white, and the bird often hides in snow banks for protection. In summer it turns brown.

Puffin - sometimes called sea parrot, is an odd-looking bird that lives in Arctic waters. It has a thick body, a large head, and a high, bright bill. The puffin "swims" underwater.

Redd - a shallow nest of gravel made by a female salmon, with her tail, in the bottom of a lake or stream. As she drops her eggs into the redd, the male fertilizes them.

Sac - a pouch-like structure on each alevin, filled with nutrients.

Scrub - is land overgrown with stunted trees or shrubs. Some of these lands occur in Alaska.

Smolt - a young, nearly adult salmon when it leaves fresh water and travels to the ocean.

Snowy Owl - The adult male is usually pure white, although it may have brown spots. Snowy owls breed in the Arctic. They live on little hills caused by frost heaves, called pingos or pingaluks.

Tundra - is a cold, dry region where trees cannot grow. Tundras are covered by snow more than half the year. Mosses, lichens, grasses, and low shrubs grow there.

27

References

Alaska Native Language Center, University of Alaska Fairbanks

Andrews, Julia L. (1991) <u>Wolves</u>. New York, New York: Bantam Doubleday Publishing Group, Inc.

Gallup, Louise (1993) <u>Owl's Secret</u>. Seattle, Washington: Sasquatch Books.

Holen, Susan D. (1988) <u>Alaska Wildlife</u>. Anchorage, Alaska: Paisley Publishing.

Holen, Susan D. (1994) <u>The Alaska Wolf</u>. Anchorage, Alaska: Paisley Publishing.

Lindstrand, Doug (2002) <u>Wild Alaska</u>. Anchorage, Alaska: Sourdough Studio

Miller, Debbie S. (1994) <u>A Caribou Journey</u>. Canada: Little Brown & Co.

Pruitt, William O., Jr. (1975) <u>The Fragile Northland: Our Magnificent Wildlife</u>.
Pleasantville, New York: The Readers Digest Association, Inc.

World Book Multimedia Encyclopedia (2001): World Book, Inc.

Alaska Department of Fish and Game

Recommendations

The best way to learn is to have fun while you are learning. <u>Alaska Animals, We Love You</u>, teaches with rhythm and accuracy, with something for both students and teachers.

Bea Rose
- of Alaska Women Speak

<u>Alaska Animals</u> is a creative and fun approach to learning. Children of all ages will have a blast chanting along with the CD, and performing the jazzy rhymes!

Amy Bridges-Williams, Playwright
- Winner of the 1997 Edward Albee Playlab Award
- Winner of the 1996 Kennedy Center Short Play Award

This book is an excellent way to introduce the music curriculum to early childhood classes.

Jolene Kearns
- Early Childhood Specialist

Alaska Animals, We Love You!

Vocals by LaVon and Alice

Guitar by Chris Basden

29